THE FLYING FINGERS CLUB

Jean F. Andrews

Kendall Green Publications
Gallaudet University Press
Washington, D.C.

Special thanks to Dr. Hal Blythe and Dr. Charles Sweet of the English Department of Eastern Kentucky University for their advice.

Kendall Green Publications
An imprint of Gallaudet University Press
Washington, DC 20002

Library of Congress Cataloging-in-Publication Data

Andrews, Jean F.
    The Flying Fingers Club/Jean F. Andrews.
        p.   cm.
    Summary: Entering a new school, Donald struggles with his learning disability and makes friends with a deaf boy who teaches him sign language and joins Donald in search for a newspaper thief.
    ISBN 0-930323-44-0
    [1. Friendship—Fiction. 2. Deaf—Fiction. 3. Learning disabilities—Fiction.   4. Physically handicapped—Fiction.]
    I. Title.
PZ7.A56725F1   1988
[Fic]—dc19   88-19875
                                                   CIP
                                                   AC

Contents

To Rachel and Sarah

CHAPTER ONE

Donald

HAPY BIRTHDAY TO MOM!

After finishing the last letter on the white cake, Donald squeezed out some more green icing from the tube and drew a flower.

"It looks good," he said to himself. "Mom will like it."

Donald Dunbar was nine years old. He was short for his age and had brown, curly hair and blue eyes. He wore glasses with round plastic frames.

Right now Donald was unhappy. He was having a hard time finding room to work in the kitchen, which was filled with boxes, some still taped shut, others half unpacked. The rest of the house was filled with boxes, too. Donald's family had just moved to Kentucky from Illinois, and he wished his mother and father would hurry up and finish unpacking. He couldn't find his baseball or his baseball bat or even his baseball cards. He hadn't met any kids yet and had no one to play with. Donald was bored.

When Donald looked up, his sister, Susan, was watching him from the kitchen doorway. Susan was always telling him what to do. Even though she was only a year older, she acted, Donald thought, as if she were at least five years older. She acted as if she were in high school.

And Susan was a brain. She was a straight-A student in the fifth grade while Donald had barely passed the third. Every day, Susan reminded Donald how smart she was and how stupid he was.

"What are *you* doing in here?" Susan asked. "Mom is going to kill you."

"None of your business, creep," replied Donald.

"Look at that mess. Green stuff all over the place. Oh, Donald. You're such a dummy. You spelled all those words wrong. At *least* you spelled 'Mom' right."

Donald had heard enough. Susan always made him feel stupid. Sometimes he thought that he hated her.

Picking up the tube of bright green icing, Donald aimed the tip at Susan's red hair. He squeezed hard and was satisfied when gooey strands of green hit their mark—one on Susan's ear and the other right on the top of her head. It looked like a big fat green worm.

"Gross! Donald, you're a stupid brat!" Susan screamed.

She took one of her schoolbooks and tossed it at her brother's head. Donald ducked and the book went crashing into the wall.

"Just what's going on here?" they heard their

mother ask. "Can't you two get along for five minutes at a time? I'm buying you both one-way tickets back to Illinois."

"That's fine with me," said Donald.

"Oh, Mother, really. Look what Donald did to me," wailed Susan. "Look at this guck in my hair. I was just standing here, minding my own business, and then he—"

"You're such a liar," yelled Donald. "You always blame me for everything!"

"I don't want to hear another word from either one of you. I know it's hard to move, but you two have got to get along better. I won't have all this fighting. . . . Why, what's this cake for?" said Mrs. Dunbar, changing the subject.

"It's your birthday cake," said Donald. "Dad bought it this afternoon and said I could decorate it."

"Oh, Mom," said Susan. "How could you eat all those misspelled words and that green icing? ICK." Susan made a face by wrinkling up her nose.

"I think it's a perfectly beautiful cake," said Mrs. Dunbar. "And Donald did a perfectly beautiful job decorating it." She gave her son a big hug and then said, "Now you two go to your rooms and unpack a few cartons while I fix dinner. And, please, have a heart. No more arguing."

After dinner, Donald and his parents sat on the porch watching the sun set. Susan had gone to her room to read. Donald couldn't understand how she could read so much. He found it pretty hard to

3

concentrate on books and didn't enjoy them much.

"Dad," said Donald, "do you think we'll be going back to Illinois again soon—I mean, before Christmas or something like that?"

"I don't think it's in the cards, son. It's already October and we just got here. You miss your buddy Jackie?"

"I miss everything," Donald said sadly. "I hate it here. Why did we have to move anyway? And school's already started and now I have to get used to a new school and I don't know anybody. It's . . . it's not fair," he blurted out.

"I agree," said his dad. "I know it's no fun for you kids to start in a new school after the semester has started. But jobs as college professors don't come up every day."

"Why did that guy have to get sick?" Donald grumbled.

"If Dr. Palmer hadn't had a slight heart attack and decided to retire early, then your mom would never have been offered the job. You know how hard she's worked to get her Ph.D. This is a wonderful opportunity for her."

Donald knew all that. Since his mother had decided to go back to school to get her advanced degree in soil science, soils and rocks seemed to be the most important thing in the Dunbar household. Bags of dirt samples with labels were all over the living room. Donald's grandmother used to say that most people swept dirt out of the house. But her daughter went out and collected it and then put it on display. Everyone in the family thought that was very funny, but not Donald.

And then his father had had to give up a perfectly good job with a computer consulting firm and find another one here in Kentucky.

"I don't want your mother to miss out on this chance," he had explained to the children back in Illinois. Then he left again to go to Kentucky to find a job for himself and a house for his family.

Mr. Dunbar had found a good job quickly. His new company helped him to find a house that was bigger than the one they had had in Illinois, with a green lawn and back porch and even an old barn. The only problem, it seemed, was Donald.

"Donald, please give this place some time," said his mother. "You'll make new friends. And look how beautiful it is." She stared out at the orange sunset.

"Why don't you go inside and write a letter to Jackie? It will make you feel better," she continued.

"Aw, Mom. You know that I hate to write."

"Please try, Donald. Jackie would like to hear from you, I know."

"Oh, Bill. What are we going to do with him?" his mother said after Donald had gone inside, unhappily dragging his feet.

"I think he may get a new start here," answered Mr. Dunbar. "And as we agreed, this time we're going to face up to his problems—and so is he."

"Well, this school *does* seem to be capable of handling a child like Donald—with a learning disability. I spoke to the principal again this morning. She went over Donald's records and test results with the special education teacher and school psychologist and they made several recommendations."

"Do they seem to know what they're talking about?" asked Mr. Dunbar.

"I think so. Donald won't be happy about it, but they suggest that he repeat the third grade. Also, to make sure that he doesn't fall farther behind, he'll work on his reading and writing skills every day in the resource room with a teacher trained to deal with learning disabilities," explained Mrs. Dunbar.

"You're right, Marilyn. Donald won't like it. But his trouble with reading is affecting everything. He's beginning to feel left out and left behind by his age group. In comparison to Susan, he's just a big baby. We've been told he can catch up. I hope he does this year."

Mrs. Dunbar sat back in her chair and watched the fading light. "It must be hard for Donald to have a sister like Susie, who reads a mile a minute. It's such a struggle for him. He sees words as if they were written backwards—in a mirror. He certainly can't spell. And he tries so hard. It's heartbreaking."

"We all just have to keep trying to help him, Marilyn. He certainly isn't stupid. Besides which, he can make lots of things with his hands. He's got real talent. We just have to get this reading thing licked," finished Mr. Dunbar.

In his bedroom, Donald tore out a piece of
paper from his notebook. He found a pencil and sat
down at his desk, staring hard at the paper.
Finally, he took a deep breath and started to write
slowly:

DEAR JAKE

I MISS YOU. I HATE
KENTUKY. MOM LIKES
THE SUNSETS. BIG DEAL.
I MISS PLAYING
BASEBALL WITH YOU,

YOUR FRIEND

DONALD

Donald was very tired when he finished. He
undressed, crawled under the covers, and lay there
with his eyes closed, wondering why sunsets were
orange. Soon he was fast asleep.

CHAPTER TWO
A Man-to-Man Talk

"Hey, Susan!" Donald yelled. "Bombs away!"

Susan looked up from the bottom of the stairs just in time to see a basket-load of dirty laundry tumble over the banister. Soon she was knee-deep in Donald's clothes—T-shirts, jeans, underwear, pajamas.

"I thought you were in a hurry for it, Sue. Seeing as it's your turn to do the laundry."

"I'm going to kill you, Donald. Just wait until it's your turn. You'll be sorry. And you can pick this stuff up by yourself and bring it into the basement." Susan gave her brother a dirty look and stamped through the door into the kitchen.

Donald heard his father's voice behind him. "Donald, you and Susan have got to stop this bickering. I think we'd all better discuss it later, but now just you and I need to have a man-to-man talk."

"Oh, brother," thought Donald. "This means trouble."

Donald and his father went into Donald's room and sat on the bed. Donald stared out the window. He could see the sun shining brightly. It was nine in the morning on a warm Saturday in October, and Donald wanted to be anyplace except where he was.

"Donald . . ." his father started slowly. "I want to talk about school. Well, your mother and I . . . we've decided that it would be better if you didn't go into a new grade just yet."

"You mean I have to be in the third grade again?" Donald asked, feeling a lump in his throat.

"Yes, you do," said his father in a low voice. "But you'll get additional help, too. The school has decided that you'll take a special class every day. Why, you'll be caught up before you know it."

"It's not fair!" Donald said angrily as he slammed his fist down on his pillow. "I want to go on to the fourth grade. And I don't want to be in a special class. Everyone will make fun of me. Those classes are for dumb kids!"

"Son, we only want what's best for you. And it's a new school. No one will even know that you've already been through the third grade. If you apply yourself this year, I bet you'll find it smooth sailing by this time next year."

Donald didn't think he'd ever have smooth sailing in school. But he did know that there was no use arguing. Sometimes it was awful being a kid. You had to do what everyone else wanted.

"Look," said his father, getting up from the bed. "We've got practically the whole weekend ahead of us. Why don't we build a new tree house out in the backyard? Better than the one we had in Illinois. What do you say?"

9

"Sure, Dad," said Donald unenthusiastically. Anything would be better than hanging around the house for two days, with nothing to look forward to except school on Monday.

Donald felt more cheerful once they got into the hardware store. There was all kinds of interesting stuff. There were bins full of shiny nails and racks with different kinds of tools. He ran his hand over the rough sandpaper on a roll near the checkout counter.

Donald and his father left the store with two bags full of nails, and screws, and sandpaper, and headed for the lumberyard to buy some pine boards.

Half an hour later, they were picking out a large oak tree with a sturdy fork in the middle of the backyard. They spent the rest of the day working on the tree house.

Donald was perfectly happy as he hammered and sawed. He was very handy with tools. He could drive a nail straight and measure a board correctly. It was only in school, with books, that he became frustrated and felt so dumb.

It was a contented Donald that went up to his room that night to get ready for bed. He noticed some piles of clean laundry that had been neatly folded and put on his bed, ready for him to put away.

"Mom! Mom!" he wailed. "Come quick!"

"Good grief," said his mother, rushing to his door. "What's the matter, Donald? What's happened?"

"Look! Look at my underwear," said Donald. "I can't believe it. It's PINK!"

"Oh, dear," said his mother. "So it is. Susan must have washed it with her red sweatpants. I told her to be careful. She must have forgotten."

"She did it on *purpose*." Donald was very upset, and went on, "Look at my Cubs T-shirt. She shrunk it and it's *pink*."

"Donald, everyone makes mistakes sometime. Your laundry isn't always perfect when it's your turn to do it."

"I don't make everything pink. I can't wear pink underwear to school. All the guys would laugh at me."

"Donald, no one is going to see your underwear. That's the point. It's *under* what you're *wear*ing," said his mother as she started to laugh.

"Mom, this isn't funny," snapped Donald. "What about my Cubs T-shirt?"

"Don't worry, sweetie. I'll get you a new one. Now, hop into bed," she said as she lightly kissed him on the forehead. "Good night and don't let the bedbugs bite."

Donald pulled his quilt up to his neck but he was still angry and couldn't fall asleep. He sat up and reached for his notebook and pencil:

ᗡƎΑЯ JΑKᴉ

I HΑVƎ Α TЯƎƎHOUSƎ

YOU GOTA COME VIZIT.
IT IS BIG, NO GIRLZ
ALOUD. ONLY BOYZ,

YOUR FRIEND

He put his notebook aside. "Yeah," he thought to himself as he looked over the letter to Jackie. "No girls allowed in *my* tree house, especially Susan!"

CHAPTER THREE
The Rescue

"Donald! Donald!"

Donald woke up as his mother called for the second time. He reached over to his bed stand and picked up his glasses. He slipped them on and headed for the second-floor landing.

"Oh, there you are, honey. It's almost eleven o'clock. I think you've overslept. Susie and your dad and I are going to look for some road cuts. Do you want to come?"

Ordinarily, Donald loved to go digging with his mother. It was fun collecting dirt samples. And he'd never known anyone who had a mother who liked to play in the dirt. Sometimes his mother's fingernails were dirtier than his. But today Donald didn't want to go.

"I want to go over to the park and see if I can find someone to play ball with, Mom. Okay?"

"Well . . . are you sure you know where the park is?"

"Mom, please, I won't get lost, I promise," said Donald impatiently.

"Okay, but, one, take your keys, two, have some

breakfast, three, be careful, and, four, we'll see you at about five o'clock."

Donald found the park easily. It was full of children roller-skating and riding bikes. Joggers ran by him and just about everybody seemed to be having a picnic. He was a little sorry that he hadn't gone with his family.

Finally, Donald noticed a group of boys playing on a baseball diamond. He rested his bat on his shoulder and walked casually toward them. He hoped they'd notice him and ask him to play. They looked older than he was, but Donald was pretty sure he could keep up.

Donald stood and watched them for a few minutes. They would call out to each other and he learned that one of them was named Pete and another Roger. No one said anything to him. He felt invisible. Finally, when Pete ran near him to pick up a ball, Donald called out, "Hey, do you guys think I could play?"

Pete stopped running and looked at Donald. "What's your name, squirt?"

"Donald."

"What grade are you in?"

"Third."

"Look. We're in the fifth grade. We don't need you and we don't play ball with wimpy little third-graders. Get lost."

Pete reached out and took Donald's baseball cap from his head. With a quick motion, he threw it as far as he could. It landed in the lower branches of a tree and just hung there. "You heard me, jerk. We don't want you here."

Donald felt close to tears, but he wasn't going to let Pete and his friends see him cry, no matter what. He turned around and walked toward the tree where his cap was stuck. He knocked it down with his bat, jammed it back on his head, and walked away without looking back.

By now, Donald was very sorry that he wasn't putting dirt in bags with the rest of his family. He wandered aimlessly through the park, and found himself in an empty, open field. He sat down with his back against what looked like a left-over sewer pipe and wondered what he should do next.

"Meow . . . meow," he heard. And then a sneeze. What was he hearing? A cat with a cold?

"Here, kitty," he called softly. "Here, cat. Where are you?"

Once again, he heard "Meow. Meow." The sound was muffled and Donald suddenly understood why. It was coming from inside the sewer pipe.

Getting down on his knees, Donald peered into the dark pipe. He couldn't see anything, but he could hear a soft meow coming from inside. Donald stretched his hand into the pipe and touched something wet and soft and furry. Gently, he pulled the tiny animal from its hiding place and took a good look at it.

In his hand was a small fur ball, a terrified cat that was probably not more than a few months old. Donald could see that it was mostly black with two white paws. Donald stroked its head, and the cat looked up at him. He had bright green eyes. The cat was also very wet and very muddy.

"He's just beautiful," Donald thought. "But he's so wet and he's shaking. I've got to get him home and dry him off."

Cradling the black cat in one arm and his bat and mitt in the other, Donald rushed home as fast as he could. The station wagon was parked in the driveway. His family was home.

"Hi, Donald," said his father as he sat at the kitchen table with Donald's mother writing out labels for their dirt samples. "You look as filthy as we do. And what's that you've got?"

"I found him in a big pipe in the park, Dad. Can I keep him? Please?"

"Now hold on a minute, Donald," said his father. "Maybe this cat already has a home."

"I'm sure he's just a lost cat," answered Donald, desperate to convince his father. "He was just lying there in the mud."

"Bill," said Mrs. Dunbar, seeing how excited her son was. "We could at least keep it for a few nights. And we could put some notices around the neighborhood and the university in case someone has lost it."

"Okay," said Mr. Dunbar. "I give up. But first order of business is a *bath*. First the cat, then you, Donald. Come on. I'll help you. Let's fill a tub in the basement with warm water and make this animal fit to live with."

Donald insisted that the cat sleep on his bed that night. His mother agreed, but said that it would only be until the cat "settled in a little bit."

The cat already had a name. Donald would call it Merlin, after the wizard in a movie he had once seen.

Before Donald went to sleep that night, he wrote another letter to Jackie.

DEAR JAKI
   I HAVE A NEW PET. HIZ
NAME IS MERLIN, HE IS
BLAK AND HAZ GREEN
EYZ. COME VIZIT to SEE
HIM.
         YOUR FRIEND
         DONALD

CHAPTER FOUR
A New Way of Talking

"Wake up, son." Donald's father stood at the doorway to his bedroom. "You've got school today. Breakfast is just about ready."

Donald sat up in bed and yawned loudly. He looked over at his windowsill. Merlin looked at him and purred loudly. Then he started to lick one paw with close attention.

Merlin was lying next to Donald's rock collection. On the windowsill next to the cat lay chunks of shiny rocks. When the sun shone on them, the way it did this morning, the glassy bits in the rocks reflected sharp points of blue, green, and yellow. Merlin lay surrounded by different colors. He really did look magical.

Donald got out of bed and quickly dressed. He picked Merlin up in his arms and went downstairs.

"Cream cheese or peanut butter for lunch?" his mother asked Donald.

"Peanut butter, please. Mom, can I take Merlin to school?"

"Of course not, Donald. I think we'll make him comfortable in the basement for today. Later, we'll decide exactly where we'll keep him. Don't worry.

He'll be waiting for you when you get home."

Donald's dad looked up from his scrambled eggs. "Are you really sure you want to take care of that cat, son?" he asked. "It's a lot of responsibility. You have to make sure that it's fed, and that it has fresh water, and make sure that it doesn't look sick. And you have to do that every single day."

"Okay, kids, let's move along. You're going to miss your bus. I've written down all the information you'll need for today," said Mrs. Dunbar. "Where your bus will pick you up to take you to and from school, and the room number where you report when you get to school. I'm sure you won't have any trouble. Well, I'm late. Don't miss your bus."

Donald did not put Merlin in the basement. He put him in his backpack. Merlin was going to school with Donald on his first day. He was sure everyone would be very interested in seeing his cat.

A yellow school bus pulled up to the corner where Donald and Susan stood. The front doors opened, and the two children with the cat got on quickly. The bus driver was busy checking the traffic, and didn't notice Merlin's head sticking out of Donald's backpack. The bus was filled with children, but for the first few minutes no one looked Merlin's way. Then a little girl with two front teeth missing who was wearing denim coveralls turned to the boy next to her.

"See the kitty," she said poking the boy hard in the ribs.

"It couldn't be. Animals aren't allowed on the bus," he said as he continued to read his comic book.

Then the girl shouted across to the tall girl who was twirling a baton in the seat next to her.

"Look at the cat. Isn't it beautiful?" she yelled over the loud voices of the other children.

"Meow, meow," mimicked the little girl as she bounced up and down in her seat.

By now, the children had noticed Donald and Susan with Merlin. The noise level in the bus became so loud that the bus driver pulled over to the side of the road.

"Now, what's going on?" he said as he turned around in the seat.

"There's a cat on the bus," someone squealed in a high-pitched voice.

The bus driver looked at Merlin, who by now was in Donald's lap.

"No cats," said the driver. "Off the bus."

"Donald's taking him to school," said Susan. She blurted out, "I think it's for some kind of science project."

Donald looked at his older sister. Even though she was usually creepy, sometimes she would surprise him when the chips were down.

"All right, all right," said the driver. "Just keep the noise down back there."

A group of third-graders let out a cheer and began bouncing in their seats. The driver glanced at his rearview mirror and started the bus.

"Where did you find him?" A young woman who

sat in front of Donald turned around and looked at the cat. A younger boy about Donald's age sat next to her and peered cautiously over the seat.

Meanwhile, Merlin moved over to the seat next to Donald and looked up at the open window.

"I found him in the park. He was lost in a big sewer."

The woman smiled, then began to make hand signals to the boy next to her. The young boy smiled and nodded.

Donald noticed the boy had plugs in his ears connected to wires that went down his shirt to a funny little box. "Must be some kind of crazy radio," thought Donald.

Susan and Donald looked puzzled. The woman laughed. "Oh," she began to explain. "This is Matt. He's deaf. His mom and dad want him to try out Lincoln Elementary public school to see if he likes it. He has been going to the state school for the deaf but wants to see how he does with hearing children. I am his interpreter."

"What's an interpreter?" asked Donald.

"An interpreter takes what you say with your voice and translates it into sign language," explained the woman. "Matt uses sign language and fingerspelling. Signs stand for ideas, and fingerspelling, well, that's when each handshape stands for the letters of the alphabet. Here, let me show you. See this sign, it means cat."

The woman made a brushing motion on the side of her face demonstrating the cat sign. "And this is the way that you fingerspell cat," she said as she

21

spelled out each letter on her fingers. "Matt can say anything with sign language that you say with your voice. By the way, my name is Terry. I am Matt's interpreter at school. My car broke down this week so I'm riding with Matt on the bus."

Matt began to sign rapidly and excitedly.

"What's he saying?" asked Susan. Both Donald and Susan had never met a person who used this new way of talking before. They were very curious.

Terry began to translate Matt's signs. She said, "He's saying the cat is escaping out the window!"

Donald and Susan quickly turned to the window.

Merlin had crawled up the back of the seat and through the bus window. He had leaped onto the street and was running straight for the park where Donald had found him. There were cars and trucks all around him.

"Oh, no!" screamed Donald. "Help! He'll be killed."

CHAPTER FIVE
Close Call

"My cat is in the middle of traffic," Donald shouted to the bus driver. "Please help him!"

Screech! Several cars stopped in the middle of the road. Merlin ran under a blue truck and across the street toward the park. He disappeared into the tall grass.

The bus driver said to Donald, "Looks like your cat made it. You'll have to look for him after school in that field. Lucky cat! I thought he was a goner."

Susan turned toward Donald. "What are you going to do now?" she asked. "You've got to go to school. You can't just run off after Merlin."

Donald slumped in his seat. He felt as if he had lost a friend. He just had to find Merlin again. He wondered if his parents would be upset because he brought the cat to school. The bus driver was mad because the cat had disrupted the ride. Now what if he were late? Maybe the teacher wouldn't want the cat in school? Donald didn't know what to do.

The bus pulled into the driveway in front of the school building. Terry and Matt got up and started walking toward the door of the bus. Matt turned to Donald and made some hand signals.

Donald looked at Terry for help. "What did he say?"

Terry interpreted. "Matt said, he hopes you find your cat."

Matt crossed both of his fingers and flashed a broad smile.

Donald crossed his fingers, too, and smiled back.

"Now, Donald," Susan warned. "Remember. Don't worry about the cat until after school."

"Yeah, kid," said the bus driver. "Forget the cat for now."

But Donald didn't go up the front steps to school. He took off toward the park. As the bell rang to start the school day, Donald headed for the concrete sewer pipe where he had found Merlin.

One hour later, Donald appeared at the school entrance. He was muddy from head to foot, and in his arms he held a black cat that was just as dirty as he was.

"Can I help you, young man?" said a stern voice.

Donald looked up and saw a woman with her arms folded. "Uh, yes, I think I should be here, or I mean I should be at school, uh," he stammered. "My name is Donald Dunbar."

"Yes, Donald, we're glad you decided to come today. I'm the principal, Mrs. Lake. You aren't exactly dressed for school, but I guess it'll have to do. Who is your friend here?" she said, pointing to Merlin.

Donald's face brightened. "This is Merlin," he said. "My cat."

"We usually don't allow students to bring in their

animals unless it's for some special occasion. But I guess your first day of school *is* a special occasion! Be sure, though, to leave him home in the future, okay? Now, go to the bathroom and get rid of some of that mud. Then come to my office—it's just around that corner."

Donald nodded.

"Let's see," said the principal when Donald returned. She scanned the computer printout showing the students' names and their room assignments. "You are in Mr. Gebhart's room. Follow me, and I'll show you where you belong."

The principal led Donald and Merlin to Mr. Gebhart's room.

"This is Donald Dunbar. He had a bit of a problem getting to school on time. But he's here now. And the cat's okay for today."

Donald and Merlin found their way to an empty desk. The other children were quietly writing in their notebooks. Donald held tightly onto Merlin. He felt nervous.

Mr. Gebhart introduced Donald to the class. "When you get more settled and comfortable, Donald, then you can tell the class all about yourself." Mr. Gebhart was looking through Donald's file. "I see that you have to go to the resource room for an hour each day. I'll show you where that is in a little while and introduce you to Mrs. Brice."

Donald looked around the classroom at all the unfamiliar faces. Across the aisle he saw Matt and Terry. She seemed upset.

"Mr. Gebhart," said Terry in a low, angry voice. "Why have you moved Matt's seat from the front of the room? You know he has to sit close so he can speechread when you talk."

"Terry, if Matt is to be part of my class, he has to follow the same rules as the other children. All students sit in alphabetical order. Matthew Morrissey must sit with the other *M*'s."

"I think it might be better if we continued this discussion in the hall," said Terry, aware of the fascinated attention of the class.

Once the door was shut behind them, Terry continued, "Mr. Gebhart, we really need your help. Matt's parents are trying to see if he can adjust to Lincoln Elementary. They want him to have as many different experiences as he can handle. They think that the special school is too limiting. Matt is very bright, you know. But he can't do it on his own."

"Terry, I don't mean to be rude, but Matt's appearance in my class has been quite a surprise. I've had no special training in teaching a hearing-impaired child. I've got twenty-five other third-graders to worry about, and several of those have some sort of learning disability. What am I supposed to do? And I also find that the other children focus on Matt and don't pay the attention they should to their own work."

"Yes, I've noticed that, too. But there must be a solution. Why don't we talk it over with the principal during recess and see what can be done?"

"I'm willing," said Mr. Gebhart. "What a

morning! I even have a black cat on my hands today."

At lunch, Donald sat alone in the cafeteria eating his peanut butter sandwich. Merlin lay curled up in his lap, sleeping. None of the other kids seemed to want to talk to him. Susan had ignored him and, anyway, he wouldn't be caught dead sitting with his sister.

Holding Merlin in his arms, Donald threw out his empty milk container and walked out to the playground.

"Hey, guys, look, it's the wimp!" he heard someone shout.

It was Pete, and Roger, and the other tough fifth-graders from the park. Donald could tell that they were the kind of kids who gave the teachers a really hard time just for the fun of it. Donald thought they were scary. Right now, they were throwing a ball around.

"Is that your kitty-cat, jerk?" asked Pete. Before Donald could stop him, he had grabbed Merlin from his owner's arms and held him high above his head.

"Who wants to play catch with this wimp's cat?" asked Pete, laughing. "Hey, Roger, coming at you!"

"You put him down," Donald screamed as loud as he could. "He's my cat. You'll hurt him!"

"What are you boys doing?" roared an adult voice. It was Mr. Gebhart, who was overseeing recess. "How dare you treat a defenseless animal that way! You return that cat right now or you'll be in detention until you're ninety!"

"Hey, man, we were only kidding," said Pete, swaggering a little as he returned Merlin to Donald. "Can't you take a joke?"

Donald didn't wait around to hear what Mr. Gebhart had to say to Pete and his friends. He held Merlin firmly in his arms and walked quickly away, looking for a quiet place where Merlin could play on the grass.

Donald saw Matt sitting on the ground by the playground fence. "Hi," he said, sitting down beside him and letting the cat loose. Merlin started to chase his tail and seemed overjoyed to be free.

Matt was a short boy with straight blond hair. He had short, stubby legs and strong arms. His hands were very small. Matt started to move his hands. He made all sorts of signals.

"Huh?" said Donald. "I don't understand those hand signs. What are you saying?"

Matt looked around in the grass. He found a short stick and pointed to a patch of dirt that was at their feet. He began scratching in the dirt with the stick.

"Oh, c-a-t spells cat," said Donald, as he spelled out the letters. "And c-u-t-e . . . What does that say?"

Matt moved two fingers up to his chin and stroked down. "Cute," he said, using his voice.

Donald had never heard a deaf voice before. He stopped and looked at Matt. It was a low-sounding voice and very difficult to understand. But with the printed word in the dirt, Donald nodded his head slowly to show he understood. "Right," he said.

"Cute cat. My cat is cute. All right, now I get you. You sure talk funny, but I understand."

At that point, a big airplane roared overhead in the clouds. Matt looked up at the airplane. "Airplane," he signed to Donald.

"Yeah, airplane," Donald said as he awkwardly tried to make his hand copy the sign that Matt had made.

Matt smiled and tossed his softball up into the air. Donald got up, too, and backed away. Matt gently tossed the ball to Donald, and Donald threw it back. It seemed forever since he and Jackie had played catch.

"Hey, I got an idea," said Donald. "Why don't you and I start our own club? We can meet in my tree house. What do you think?"

"Huh?" said Matt. He did not understand Donald's talk at all. It was very hard to lipread him because he talked so fast.

Donald knelt down, picked up a stick, and began to write and draw in the dirt.

DONALD + MAT = KLVZ IN 🌳 🏠

Matt's face brightened. He made the sign for friend, then touched Donald on the shoulder and his own shoulder. He bent down and corrected Donald's writing. He wrote over it:

DONALD + MAT = KLVZ IN 🌳 🏠

When the bell rang signaling the end of recess, Donald motioned to Matt and the boys walked together into the school building.

That night, Donald sat on a stool in the kitchen talking to his mother while she mixed cake batter with a fork.

"Mom, I met this kid at school today. He sounds funny and he talks with his hands. He's got these weird plugs in his ears, too. What's wrong with him?"

His mother picked up some batter with her finger and tasted it while she thought about Donald's question. "I bet he's deaf, Donald, that's what *I* think."

"That's what this lady named Terry said on the bus, too. But this kid can hear airplanes. He heard them on the playground and looked up even before I did."

"Well, maybe he can hear loud, outside noises okay," she said as she added more butter to the cake batter. "He must be using sign language. You know, you've seen it on TV. His voice sounds different because he can't hear his own voice. What's his name?"

"Matt," answered Donald. "We're going to start a club in my tree house," he added enthusiastically.

"Terrific," said his mother. "I have all sorts of projects around the house that your club can take care of like weeding the roses, raking leaves, emptying the garbage . . ."

"Mom! Not that kind of club. This one is for fun!"

"Oh," said his mother. "Do club members, by any chance, like to lick cake bowls?" she asked as she poured the batter from the mixing bowl to the cake pan.

"Sure!" said Donald. "Here, I'll show you," he said as he took the mixing bowl and stuck his finger into the remaining buttery mixture.

CHAPTER SIX
Flashing Lights

"But, Mom, why can't I?" asked Donald in a whining voice.

"Because I don't know Matt's parents. Why don't you invite Matt over here for dinner? I enjoy having him here," answered his mother as she wiped the kitchen table with a sponge.

"Your mother and I would feel more comfortable if we knew Matt's parents, that's all," explained his father.

It was a Saturday morning and Donald was sitting in the kitchen arguing with his mother and father. Matt's family had invited Donald to have dinner with them that evening. Matt had reminded Donald about the dinner invitation on Friday afternoon before Donald got off the bus.

Seeing her son's disappointment, Mrs. Dunbar said, "Why don't I give them a call on the phone? That'll make me feel better about this."

"But, Mom, you can't call them," answered Donald, throwing his hands up in exasperation.

"Why not? Don't they have a phone?" she asked.

"Mom, they're deaf," said Donald.

"His parents are deaf, too?" said his mother. "You

didn't tell me that." She stopped cleaning the table and sat on a chair to follow the conversation more intently.

"What does it matter?" asked Donald. "What difference does it make?"

"How can they take care of Matt?" she said. "And what about you? I wouldn't feel comfortable having you . . ."

"Matt has a baby sister, too. Real little. Cries and everything," answered Donald.

"Oh, my," said his mother as she took off her orange checkered apron. "I don't like the sound of this at all. The answer is no, Donald. Not tonight. Not until we meet his parents. Get to know them better. I didn't realize that the whole family was . . . was . . . was like that."

Mr. Dunbar was emptying the dishwasher and stacking the dishes in the cupboard. He had been quiet for most of the conversation but now began to talk.

"I think we're really making a big deal out of nothing. Good grief! We know Matt very well. He goes to Donald's school and seems to come from a nice family. Why don't we drive Donald over and just drop in and meet Matt's family? We don't have to stay long. That way you'll be reassured, Marilyn, that Donald'll be safe. There are two deaf workers at my company, you know. I don't know them very well but they seem to be like other people. They just communicate with their hands rather than voices."

Donald's mother looked at her son. "Okay, I give

in. But I guess it would make me feel better if we at least could get a look at them," she said.

"Whoopee!" yelled Donald. He threw his arms around his mother.

That afternoon, at around four-thirty Donald and his parents and Susan got into the car and drove three blocks to the Morrissey home. In the car, Donald's mother began to worry.

"How will we talk with them if they are deaf?" she asked.

"Don't worry, Mom," said Donald. "Matt and I will help you out." He had learned a lot of signs from Matt and he found that now he could say simple things with his hands.

"Marilyn," her husband said impatiently. "Don't you think they know how to write?"

When they arrived at Matt's house, Donald ran up the sidewalk and he pushed the doorbell. In less than a minute, the door opened and a man smiled at them. He began to use sign language and motioned the group into the house. Soon a woman and Matt joined him.

"Dad, he is saying that he's happy to meet you," interpreted Donald.

"Oh, we're happy to meet you, too," said Donald's mother and father nervously as each extended their right hand.

"How did you know the doorbell was ringing?" signed Donald to Matt.

Matt smiled and pointed to the light in the living room, then signed, "We have lights in the kitchen and in the bedrooms that tell us when the doorbell rings. See the light on the wall? When you press the doorbell, then we see three slow flashes," Donald explained what Matt had said.

"Neat!" said Susan.

"Donald, tell Matt's parents that we are very happy that they invited you to dinner," said his father.

"Dad," said Donald, "I can't interpret all that. It's too much."

Mr. Morrissey came to the rescue. He pulled a pad and pencil out of a desk drawer. He quickly began to write.

My wife and I appreciate your letting Matt come over to your house to play with your son. We are happy he has found some hearing friends.

He handed the pad to Donald's father. Mrs. Dunbar leaned over her husband's shoulder and read the message. Then both parents smiled and nodded at the deaf couple.

Donald's father wrote back.

You are very welcome. Matt is a nice boy. Have you lived in this neighborhood long? Our family moved here from Illinois in October. Marilyn, my wife, is a professor of soil science at the university and I work for a computer firm.

Mr. Morrissey answered:

We've lived in this neighborhood for three years now. My wife and I work in a laboratory for a medical company. We like the neighborhood. It's a good place for kids to play in.

A baby began to cry. Regular on-off flashes from a light in a back bedroom reflected off the side living room wall near the hallway. Matt's father looked at his wife. He said, "Jessie?"

Matt began to sign. "That's my baby sister, Jessie."

Matt's mother ran out of the room and returned in a few minutes with a baby in her arms.

"Oh, she's so cute," said Susan as she looked at the baby.

"Do you babysit?" signed Matt's mother to Susan.

"Donald, what did she say?" asked Susan.

When Donald interpreted, Susan answered Matt's mom. "Yes, I can baby-sit during afternoons. But my parents don't let me baby-sit late at night."

Suddenly, the light bulb flashed in the living room as well as in the other rooms in the house. The group could see three quick light flashes bounce off the walls of the hallway.

"Now, what?" asked Mrs. Dunbar.

"Must be the phone," signed Matt's father. "Come, let me show you," he signed as he motioned them to the kitchen.

When they went into the kitchen, a light on the kitchen wall was flashing. Matt's father picked up the phone receiver and put it on top of a small rectangular box that looked like a typewriter. He sat down and began to type.

HELLO MORRISSEY HERE GA

On the top of the typewriter, words began to come out over the read-out panel.

HELLO DAVE JIM HERE CALLED TO TELL YOU
DEAF CLUB MEETING CANCELED ON SUNDAY WILL

RESCHEDULE IT NEXT WEEK MAYBE IF WEATHER
PERMITS GA

Matt's father then responded by typing in a
message.

THANKS JIM DEPOSITED LAST WEEKS DUES IN
BANK TODAY WILL SEND YOU SLIP GA

Again, a reply came over the typewriter.

GREAT DAVE SEE YOU NEXT WEEK SOMETIME
HAVE A NICE WEEKEND GA TO SK

And Matt's father typed,

SAME TO YOU JIM SK SK

Matt's father hung up the phone receiver on the
wall and turned off the typewriter. He picked up
the pad of paper and wrote a note to Donald's
parents.

*This is a telecommunications device or a TDD.
Deaf people use it to telephone each other. I'm
treasurer of our local deaf club and Jim is the
president. He just called about a meeting cancella-
tion. GA means that the other person "goes ahead"
with the message. SK SK means we're through
talking and we're signing off.*

By now the baby was squirming in her mother's
arms. Taking this as a cue, Donald's mother said, "I
think we'd better be going now, looks like a hungry
baby!"

Donald signed to Matt and his parents that his
parents had to go.

Donald's father said, "Son, we'll pick you up
about eight o'clock." As he said this, he held up
eight fingers and pointed to the clock on the
kitchen wall.

After they had left, everyone went into the kitchen. Matt's mother put Jessie into the high chair and began to stir the pots of food on the stove.

"Ba, ba, ba," Jessie said. "Ga, ga, ga," she continued as she picked up her spoon and banged it on the wooden table of her high chair.

"Put her bib on," signed Matt's mother to him, "and you and Donald can set the table."

"Ma ma," signed Jessie as she made a fist and hit her chin.

"Can she sign?" asked Donald.

"Yes, but she uses mostly baby signs," signed Matt to Donald. "Sometimes she doesn't make them right. She can hear, too."

"Jessie wants to eat?" signed her mother as she looked at her daughter.

"Eeeeeeeeeeeeeeeeeeeeeee," screeched Jessie. Then she put all her fingers in her mouth.

"I think she's hungry," said Matt's father.

The family all sat down and Matt's mother began to pass the food. Donald helped himself to a plate of beef stew. When the biscuits came around, he took one.

"Now don't be shy," signed Matt's father as he motioned him to take more.

Donald smiled and took two more. He loved biscuits.

After everyone had filled their plates, Donald noticed an interesting thing. Everyone was signing and eating at the same time. Even Jessie. In his house, dinnertime was spent talking about what had happened at school or work. Everyone talked.

Especially Susan. You just couldn't keep her quiet. But his mother always reminded them not to talk with food in their mouth. At Matt's house, they could talk and eat at the same time because everyone signed.

Matt began to complain to his parents. "I don't like the hearing school. Donald is my only friend. I want to go back to the deaf school."

Matt's mother signed, "Your father and I thought it would be better for you to try the hearing school. Then you can be at home with us, instead of living there. At least stick it out until June."

"Please, Mom," signed Matt to his mother. "I hate it there. I like the deaf school. I want to be with my deaf friends."

Donald was stunned. He knew that Matt was not always happy at school, but he didn't know that he felt so strongly about it.

Matt's father signed, "We thought you should at least have the chance of going to a hearing school. Your teachers say you are having a hard time. Isn't your interpreter helping you enough?"

"Terry is nice and she helps me a lot," signed Matt. "But I miss my deaf friends and all the fun we had in the dorms. And I miss drama club."

Donald signed, "We have drama club at Lincoln. You can join that."

Matt went on, "But it's not the same. At Lincoln, the drama club is all hearing. They get the best parts. I can't because I can't hear. At the deaf school, all actors are deaf so I have more of a chance."

Matt's father signed, "Why don't you stay until June? Then, if you want to go back to the deaf school, we will discuss it again. Your mother and I both went to deaf schools, but we wanted you to have the chance to try out the hearing school."

Matt signed, "Do I have to wait so long?"

"Yes, you do," signed his mother.

To change the subject, Matt's father suggested, "Why don't we watch the news on TV?"

"Not until you help me clear the table and wash the dishes," signed Matt's mother.

After the kitchen was cleaned up, the family and Donald went into the den and watched TV. Matt opened the drawer and pulled out a deck of cards. "Do you want to play Go Fish?" he asked Donald.

"Sure," signed Donald.

Donald looked at the television screen and noticed that on the bottom of the screen were words! There were lots of words in a black box.

"What's that?" he asked Matt.

"We can't hear voices talking, so we read the words," signed Matt. "Here, cut the deck and deal," he signed, then handed the cards to Donald.

"Can you read all those words?" asked Donald, as he began to deal out the cards.

"Some I can," signed Matt. "But not all. Sometimes my Mom and Dad interpret for me. They explain the words to me. Do you have any queens?"

"Go Fish," said Donald. "Do you have any kings?"

Matt handed Donald a king.

The boys played several games of Go Fish, and at

40

about a quarter to eight, three slow flashing lights went on in the den. Someone was at the front door.

It was Mrs. Dunbar. She thanked the Morrisseys again for inviting her son and motioned Donald to the car.

"Good-bye. Thank you very much," signed Donald to Matt and his family. "Matt, I'll see you on Monday."

When they got into the car, Donald's father, who was waiting in the driver's seat, asked him about his evening.

"It was fun," said Donald.

"What did you do?" asked his mother.

"We ate and talked. Then watched some TV and played cards. Matt has a funny TV," he said.

"What do you mean, a funny TV?" asked his mother with curiosity.

"Well, it has a black box on top of it. And on the screen is a black space with white words in it that you read so you know what the people are saying."

"That must be a captioning device," said Mr. Dunbar, as he pulled up in front of their house. "You know, Marilyn, before some shows they sometimes have written that 'this show is closed-captioned for the hearing impaired,'" he said.

"Daddy, what does 'closed-captioned' mean?" Donald asked.

"Well, the black box on top of the TV is a device called a decoder. It lets people read captions on the TV screen. The signal is carried invisibly by the networks and only when the decoder is on can you see the captions. So if the network wants, they can caption, or write out in words, what the actors are saying on TV. That way the hearing-impaired population or deaf people can enjoy TV."

"We're home," said his mother. "I like the Morrisseys, don't you, Bill? Maybe we can invite them over sometime. I still feel a little uncomfortable around sign language, though. I guess you get used to it. You certainly have picked it up, Donald," she said affectionately to her son.

"I like it. It's fun. . . . I really hope Matt stays at Lincoln," he continued.

"Oh, is he thinking about leaving?" asked his mother.

"He doesn't like it there. He says he misses his deaf friends," said Donald.

"Well, I can understand that," said his father. "We tend to feel more comfortable around people who are most like us."

"Not me," said Donald as he opened the front door. "I like people who are different."

Donald scooped up Merlin, who was curled at the foot of the stairs, and carried him up to his room. That night Donald dreamed in sign language, but he couldn't understand the signs.

CHAPTER SEVEN
Who Stole the News- papers?

"Yes, this is the Dunbar residence," said Mrs. Dunbar as she listened to the voice on the kitchen phone. "Susan is right here. Just a minute, please."

"Susan, I think it's one of your customers," she said and handed the receiver across the table to where Susan sat eating her breakfast.

"This is Susan." Susan listened to the man on the line. Her face became white. "But, I *did* deliver your paper this morning," she said. "You don't have to yell, Mr. Saunders. I'll get you another paper." She put down the receiver.

"Daddy, I just don't know what is happening. That's the fourth call I've gotten this morning. Everything seems to go just fine until Sunday!" she exclaimed.

"Boy, are you in trouble now," said Donald as he knelt on the floor and petted Merlin. Susan glared at him.

"Are the calls from people in the same neighborhood?" her father asked as he stirred his coffee.

"Yes," Susan said. "They all live in the condo complex across from the park." Her voice became shrill. "I just don't understand it! I think the condo complex is jinxed. I park my bike and deliver each paper to the front door and for the third Sunday in a row, they've been stolen."

"Susan, your mother is getting tired of these irate calls from disgruntled customers. And to tell you the truth, I'm not happy about buying fifteen dollars' worth of newspapers each Sunday. Maybe you should think of giving up the paper route. It's turning into a lot of trouble."

"Oh, please, Daddy," said Susan. "I wanted to buy everyone nice Christmas presents this year. And there are only three weeks to Christmas and I still don't have nearly enough."

Susan had insisted on starting a paper route the very week that they had moved to Kentucky. She said that it would help her find her way around town.

"Let's be calm, honey," said Susan's father. "Start at the beginning and tell us everything that happened today."

"Just like every morning, I got up at six when my alarm clock went off. I got dressed and grabbed my *Herald Times* white canvas bag. I took an apple from the refrigerator and went outside to pick up the bundle of papers. I rolled each one, put rubber bands around them and put them in the plastic bags, and—"

"I know," interrupted Donald. "Why don't you put some bugging devices in the papers. Then you can find out where they end up!"

"Donald, get serious!" said Susan. "And let me

finish. Then I put the forty-five rolled newspapers in my bag, jumped on my ten-speed, and went on my delivery route. When I got to the condo, which is my last stop, I parked my bike, then walked with the papers into the building and delivered them all."

"Did you notice anybody up when you delivered the papers?" asked her mother.

"Sure," answered Susan. "Some people are always out jogging or walking their dogs."

"Has anyone ever followed you or did you pass anyone that looked peculiar?" asked her father.

"No." Susan stopped and thought. "I don't remember ever seeing anyone creepy."

Mr. Dunbar drank the last of his coffee. "Susan, let's go over to the condo, deliver the papers, and talk to some of your customers. Maybe someone has seen something."

Despite Susan and her father's inquiries at the condo complex, they could find out no information about the missing papers. Some of the residents were sympathetic, but others were angry because they had received their newspapers several hours late on Sundays. Three people canceled their subscriptions.

Seeing his daughter's disappointment, Mr. Dunbar said, "Why don't we stop at the Bluegrass Diner for some ice cream?"

Susan and her father sat at the red stools at the counter of the diner. The waitress took their order and then noticed Susan's newspaper delivery bag.

"I hope you're not selling newspapers, honey,

we've already bought and sold ours. A kid comes around."

Susan looked at her dad. "You already bought yours?" they said at the same time. But by then the waitress had left to go to the kitchen to place their orders. A different waitress brought out the bowls of ice cream. When Susan's father asked to see the other waitress, the manager told them that she had left for the afternoon.

"Well, maybe *you* know something about where you get the morning newspapers being sold here," Mr. Dunlap asked.

"Nope, don't know a thing. I'm the afternoon manager," he answered. "Look, I gotta go now. Enjoy."

That night at dinner, Susan and her dad described the strange happenings at the Bluegrass Diner.

"When Jackie comes to town," said Donald, "he and Matt will help you solve this mystery. Jackie can still come visit, can't he?" asked Donald.

"Sure," said Mrs. Dunbar. "Right after Christmas would be perfect. We'll all be home for vacation."

Donald was excited. He had not seen his friend for several months. Before he went to sleep he wrote:

DEAR JAKE,
COME VIZIT! AFTER
X-MAS WILL BE FINE.

SOMEONE IS STEELING
SUSAN'S NEWSPAPERS.
WE NEED HELP.
HURY COME. MY MOM
WILL CALL YOUR MOM.

YOUR FRIEND
DONALD

47

CHAPTER EIGHT
Jackie's Visit

"When did you say that Jackie's flight was arriving?" whispered Mr. Dunbar to his wife.

"On the afternoon of the twenty-eighth. At least that's what his mother was planning," she whispered back. "She said she'd call us after Christmas to confirm the day and time."

Donald's parents sat in the school auditorium. It was the evening of Lincoln Elementary's Christmas pageant. Somewhere behind the curtains were Susan and Donald. Susan was to be an angel in the Nativity scene and Donald was in the Christmas chorus. Donald had volunteered Merlin for the barn scene, but this idea, to his disappointment, was vetoed by Mr. Primm, the glee club director.

"Oh, look!" said Mrs. Dunbar. "They're beginning now. The curtain is opening. Oh, good grief, it's stuck!"

Finally, the curtain opened after a short delay. The children reenacted the birth of Christ in Bethlehem. On the side stood Terry, who was interpreting the whole presentation. After this scene was over, a chorus of boys and girls dressed in neat white blouses and dark skirts or pants paraded onto the stage.

"Look," said Mr. Dunbar to his wife. "There's Matt. I wonder what he's doing there?"

When the chorus began to sing out loud and use sign language for "Silent night, holy night, all is calm, all is bright," Donald's father's question was answered. After the chorus sang and signed several more songs, everyone went across the hall to the cafeteria for punch and cookies.

"See?" signed Donald to Matt. "Everyone wants to learn sign." Donald then reached for a Christmas cookie and began licking off the silver candies.

"Sure," signed Matt. "They'll learn just a few signs in songs but they never use it with me in school. Some kids talk a little bit to me on the playground, but when it gets too hard, they just give up. I like the deaf school better. There everyone knows sign. Here only a few know signs. Really, just you and Terry. I miss my deaf friends. Hearing school is boring."

Donald shrugged his shoulders and crammed the remainder of the cookie into his mouth. Matt sure complained a lot, he thought. He tried to change the subject. "Hey, my friend Jackie is visiting me from Illinois after Christmas. You'll come over, won't you?"

"Sure," signed Matt. "Can we go up in the tree house?"

"If it's not too cold," signed Donald. "It really gets windy up there. And now it's full of snow. Maybe we can shovel it off." Donald was very proud of the tree house. He and his dad had finished it just a couple of days before Thanksgiving. It looked great!

"Got to go now," Matt signed as he saw his father signal him at the door. "Talk to you later."

The next few days were very busy around the Dunbar house. Donald's parents decorated the house with holly and evergreens. The children helped them string popcorn and paper chains around the six-foot fir tree they put up in the living room. To Donald, it looked as if there were a thousand ornaments on the tree.

Christmas day was wonderful, with presents and a turkey dinner and sledding, but by the time Jackie arrived three days later, Donald was ready for a change. He and Susan were getting into too many fights. They got along better when they spent their days away from each other in school.

Jackie arrived on Saturday afternoon. It was exciting for Donald to go to the airport with his parents to pick him up. Donald could pick out Jackie the minute he got off the plane. He still had red hair, of course, and he was still chubby. Jackie liked to eat. So did Donald, but he never could put on weight. Donald often wished he wasn't so short and skinny. He'd like to have more muscles. Then maybe the bigger boys at school wouldn't pick on him!

Matt was going to come over to join the boys later. Donald had written to Jackie about sign language and his new friend Matt. Jackie was curious.

"What'll I say to him?" asked Jackie as he put a second fudge and marshmallow cookie in his mouth. The boys had just started a game of

Monopoly and lay on their stomachs on the floor of the den.

"Just act like you usually act," answered Donald. "It's no big deal or anything. You probably won't understand his voice until you are around him more. I'll interpret for you at first until you can learn some signs."

Jackie felt a little bit jealous. Donald knew how to do something that he didn't even know about. Jackie always hated it when Donald beat him at games. Winning was more fun.

"Donald, Donald," his mother called from the kitchen. "Matt is here."

Donald went to get Matt. "This is my friend, Jackie," he signed to Matt.

Matt signed hello to Jackie.

Jackie paused a minute. He felt nervous around Matt and Donald. He had never seen people sign before except on TV. It looked very strange. When Matt began to talk, Jackie got even more nervous. He couldn't understand him very well. He didn't know what to do or say.

"Let's finish our game," signed Donald. "I roll next." Donald took the die and rolled them across the board. The other boys sat down near the game board and relaxed a bit.

Donald and Jackie played intently for a while and talked back and forth to each other, excluding Matt. "OOee, look!" shouted Donald. "I landed on Park Place. I'm going to buy it to go with Boardwalk. Then I'll put houses and motels here and wipe you clean, Jackie." Donald clapped his hands.

Donald and Jackie continued talking to each other. Matt looked at the two boys quickly moving their lips and he could not understand what they were saying. He was mad. He felt left out. "Donald prefers Jackie to me," he thought.

"Oh, no. I landed in jail," said Donald. He looked up at Matt and saw that he was about to cry. "What's wrong?" he signed.

"I'm going home," signed Matt angrily. "I don't want to be here with stupid hearing people. Talk, talk, talk, that's all you do. It bores me to death!" Matt stomped out of the room.

Donald felt bad. It *was* so much easier to talk with Jackie than with Matt. With Jackie, he didn't have to think, talk, and sign at the same time. But he knew he should have paid better attention to Matt.

"Wait, Matt, come back," he said. But by then Matt had grabbed his coat and walked through the back door, slamming it on the way out. Matt headed straight for the tree house.

"C'mon, Jackie. We ought to go after him."

By the time the boys had put on their coats and run to the tree house, Matt was up in it with a pile of snowballs in front of him.

"Pow!" A cold, icy snowball hit Donald in the head. "Pow, pow!" Two more snowballs hit Jackie.

The boys threw snowballs back and forth until they were laughing at each other. "Give up?" Donald signed up to Matt.

"Yes, yes, yes," signed Matt as he moved his fist back and forth. Donald and Jackie climbed the rope ladder to their tree house fort. As they got halfway up, Matt dumped a bucketful of snow on them. The boys shook it off, then climbed the last few steps into the wooden tree house. They were all laughing very hard.

Once they were settled inside, Donald said, "I'm sorry Matt. It's just that signing gets too hard sometimes. It's easier for me to talk. I promise to sign when you're here. Really, I'll try."

"Promise?" asked Matt.

"Cross my heart and hope to die," signed Donald.

"Is this your clubhouse?" asked Jackie. "I like it. What are all these rubber bands doing here?" He reached under a shelf and into a cardboard shoe box and pulled out a fistful of rubber bands.

Donald interpreted what Jackie had said to Matt. Then he continued, "Those are for rubber band fights on the playground when the weather gets warmer. They're extras from Susan's paper route. Remember, I wrote you about that?"

"Yeah," said Jackie. "Did you ever find the person who was swiping her newspapers?"

"No," said Donald.

"I think we should investigate," said Jackie. "That's what they do on TV, you know. We need to find some clues. Hey, you got anything to eat up here?"

A few seconds later the boys were in the kitchen, headed straight for the peanut butter jar.

"If the papers only get stolen on Sundays, maybe we should all follow Susan on her route tomorrow and see if we can find any more clues," said Jackie.

The boys agreed to meet the next day with their bikes. Jackie could borrow Mr. Dunbar's old three-speed.

Bright and early the next morning, Donald, Matt, and Jackie stood around Susan as she busily wrapped her newspapers. "Are you sure you want to do this?" asked Susan.

"Yeah, sure we are," answered Donald.

"Well, first of all, help me wrap these papers," said Susan. The three boys helped her, and within ten minutes all forty-five papers were done.

"Oh, Donald," exclaimed Susan. "You are so clumsy. You folded these all wrong. Look, they should be tucked in this way," said Susan with exasperation. "But it's too late now. I'll just have to deliver them like this."

"Picky, picky, picky," said Donald. He stuck his tongue out at his sister.

"Okay, forget it. Why don't you meet me at the condo complex in about thirty minutes. Then you can watch and see if anybody comes and steals the papers. There are some bushes near the side entrance. That would be a good place to hide your bikes."

A half hour later, the boys headed for the condo. They parked their bikes behind the bushes and hid themselves. Donald took along his binoculars in case he climbed a tree to get a better look.

"If anyone sees anything suspicious, then give a whistle," said Jackie.

"Wait a minute," said Donald. "Matt can't hear.

I know, if you see anything, Matt, then you can throw a stick in the air. That'll be your signal," signed Donald.

Donald climbed a tree with the binoculars and looked at a Kentucky bluebird and a red cardinal perched on a branch in the winter sun. Jackie sat behind a bush at the side of the building. He reached into his pocket and pulled out a candy bar. Matt was in the front of the building behind an evergreen bush.

The boys watched Susan walk into the building with the final fifteen papers of her route. About ten minutes later, she left the building. The boys waited and waited but nothing happened. Just as Donald slid down the tree to join Jackie, he saw a bike pull up to the apartment complex. A boy with a red ski mask got off and went into the building. He was carrying an empty tan knapsack. Donald and Jackie looked at each other, wondering what to do next.

About ten minutes later, the boy in the red ski mask left the building with newspapers bulging from his backpack. The boys saw a stick go into the air. Matt's signal! The thief saw Matt come from behind the bushes, so he jumped on his bike and started pedaling quickly down the street.

"After him!" yelled Jackie.

"What is Matt doing?" said Donald with exasperation. "Why isn't he coming?"

Matt was on all fours crawling around in the bushes. He was pushing the snow aside in piles as if he was looking for something. Donald and Jackie pulled their bikes out of the bushes and rode over toward Matt.

"Hurry up, Matt!" yelled Jackie.

"He can't hear you," said Donald.

"Now we'll never catch the thief," said Jackie. "This deaf kid is too slow!"

"I thought I saw something fall out of the kid's pocket. Something shiny. I saw it out of the corner of my eye," signed Matt.

"Well, while you were wasting your time playing in the snow," said Jackie sarcastically, "the thief got away!" It was probably a good thing that Matt wasn't looking at Jackie's lips when he said that.

Matt pulled his bike out of the bushes and joined the other two boys. When they got to the street, they had lost the thief. The boys rode around the park several times looking for him. They were terribly disappointed.

"Well, do you think we should give up and go home?" asked Donald.

"Let's go get something to eat first," Jackie suggested.

"Good grief, you are always hungry," signed Donald.

"I could use something too," said Matt. Let's go to the Bluegrass. I want a hot dog."

"Me too," signed Donald.

"I bet I could eat six of 'em," said Jackie.

The boys rode over to the Bluegrass Diner. It was crowded on this late Sunday morning, serving breakfast to the late churchgoers. The boys entered the diner and sat at the counter near the cash register. Several men sat on the other stools reading the Sunday paper.

"Can I help you boys?" asked the waitress as she handed them a menu.

"We each want two hot dogs, please, with chili sauce," said Donald. It was the Bluegrass Diner's specialty. The chili sauce was homemade. "And some Cokes, too."

The waitress took back the menus and put them in a stack near the cash register.

"What's the sign for dumbbell?" Jackie asked Donald.

Donald touched his fist to his head several times. Jackie mimicked the sign to Matt. "You are a dumbbell," he signed in an exaggerated way. "You let the thief get away!"

"Well, you are a pea brain," Matt signed back. "And a big fatso," he continued, but this time with real anger in his eyes. "You could have chased the robber yourself if you weren't so fat!"

"Knock it off, you two," signed Donald. "Did you find anything on the ground, Matt?" he asked.

"No, nothing," signed Matt disappointedly. "I thought maybe he dropped his jackknife or some money. There was something shiny, I'm sure of it."

The boys sat quietly while waiting for their orders to come.

"Look!" signed Matt excitedly. "Look at those newspapers."

"What about them?" asked Jackie while Donald interpreted.

Then Jackie and Donald looked at each other. Several of the newspapers were folded differently. In fact, they were folded just like the ones that Donald had prepared for Susan that morning, which had annoyed her so much.

The waitress returned with three Cokes on a tray. "Here you are, boys," she said. "Your hot dogs are on the way."

"Those newspapers," said Donald. "Over there. Are they for sale?" he asked.

"Yeah," the waitress replied. "It'll cost you a buck each."

"Where did you get them?" asked Jackie.

"From the newspaper people, where else?" said the waitress in an abrupt tone. "What is this, twenty questions or something?"

"We're just interested in being newspaper delivery boys, that's all," said Jackie to reassure her.

"Well, we already have one here. We have a kid who sells us the Sunday papers every week. . . . That's the bell. Your dogs must be up," she said and hurried back to the kitchen to get the boys' order.

Donald sipped his Coke. "The thief has been here with the goods," he signed. "But how will we catch him?"

"Maybe if we talk with the manager?" asked Jackie.

"We need more clues," signed Matt. "We know it's a boy on a bike with a red ski mask and a tan knapsack and that he's selling the papers here. But we don't have any suspects."

The boys finished their hot dogs and returned home to talk to Susan and Donald's parents about what had happened that morning.

"Good work, boys," said Donald's father. "Susan and I thought something fishy was going on at the Bluegrass Diner, too."

"I wish I didn't have to go home tomorrow," said Jackie. "I really want to stay and help you solve this mystery."

Matt went with Donald and his parents to take Jackie to the airport the next day.

"I'll miss you," said Donald.

"I'll miss you, too. And you, too, Matt," he said as he awkwardly waved good-bye.

Matt smiled back. But it was not a friendly smile. He was secretly glad that Jackie was leaving. "Now Donald will pay more attention to me," he thought.

"I'll write and tell you what happens," said Donald.

CHAPTER NINE

The Attack on the Flying Fingers Club

One warm March afternoon, Donald and Matt lay on their backs in the tree house. Merlin lay in the sun, too, licking his whiskers. The newspaper thief was not stealing papers every Sunday now, so the boys were unable to find any new clues. Matt and Donald had gone back to the Bluegrass Diner to ask more questions about who was selling the Sunday newspapers to them, but no one knew anything more.

Despite a few arguments now and then, Donald and Matt had become the best of friends in and out of school. Things were a little better at school for both of them. Donald was making good progress in reading and writing with Mrs. Brice in the resource room. He had learned to use the computer, and with Mrs. Brice's help had written several stories on it.

Mr. Gebhart had permitted Matt to sit in the front of the room, although Matt still had a difficult time speechreading him. Terry had convinced the principal that teachers needed to know more about deafness at Lincoln Elementary.

Terry was trying to help Matt keep up in class. But Matt was still left out of many class discussions because by the time he could turn around and see who was talking, a different person had started. When Terry tried interpreting each student's response, Matt would get mixed up as to who was saying what. Terry thought perhaps she could ask Mr. Gebhart to arrange the desks in a semicircle, but decided not to because she didn't see how they *could* make a semicircle for twenty-five pupils! Matt was still unhappy and bored in school and often complained to his parents and Donald.

Matt had difficulties, too, outside of class. Sometimes the other kids at school would forget that he was deaf and try to get his attention when he wasn't looking at them. And when he didn't respond, they thought he was stuck-up. He also missed many social opportunities to talk in the hallways or in the cafeteria because no one knew sign language well—the little sign language that the students had used during the Christmas pageant was now forgotten.

But Matt had found a true friend in Donald, and had taught him a great many signs and the manual alphabet. Donald liked to spell words with his fingers. Sometimes when he was watching TV, he would fingerspell the words on the commercials.

And when he was sitting at the breakfast table, he would spell out the words on cereal boxes, milk cartons, and other food labels. But best of all he liked signing. His favorite sign was the one for cat.

"I wonder what we should call our club?" thought Donald idly, as he peeled a banana. "What would be a good name?" Donald petted Merlin's fur. "You know, Matt," he said as he threw his banana peel over his shoulder onto the tree house floor, "our club needs a name and we need some money to do things—like solve the newspaper mystery." He then fingerspelled "k-l-u-b."

"Yes," replied Matt in sign language as he nodded.

"Hey," said Donald, sitting up. "Look at all those birds." A large flock of birds flew over the treetop. There must have been hundreds of blackbirds filling the sky. "I know," said Donald. "What about the Bird Club?"

"No," signed Matt rapidly. "We don't watch birds, we do other things."

"Your fingers sure fly all over the place when you use that sign language," said Donald. "Hey, that's an idea. How about the Flying Fingers Club?"

"Huh?" said Matt. Sometimes Donald talked so fast and used so few signs that Matt could not understand him clearly.

Donald fingerspelled slowly. F-l-i-i-n-g F-i-n-g-e-r K-l-u-b. Despite his misspellings, Matt understood.

"Oh, the Flying Fingers Club. I like that."

"Donald. Donald, are you up there?" called a voice from the back porch.

Donald poked his head over the side of the tree house. "Yeah, Mom," he answered.

"Donald, I'm running to the store and will be back in about an hour. Your father should be home soon. Susie's Girl Scout troop just finished their meeting in the living room, so you kids are home alone. See you in a little bit."

"Hey, Mom. Would you mail that letter I wrote to Jackie for me? It's on my nightstand near my bed." Donald had written Jackie that no new clues in the newspaper case had turned up.

No sooner had Donald's mother pulled out of the driveway, then SPLAT! A big red balloon filled with water exploded on the floor of the tree house. Suddenly, water splashed all over the boys, and Merlin as well.

MEOW! MEOW! Merlin, who was sitting beside Donald, jumped out of the tree house onto a limb nearby. He did not like to get his fur wet.

"What's going on?" yelled Donald.

Donald heard some giggles in the bushes near the tree.

"Susan," he called. "Is that you?"

SPLAT! Another water balloon landed on the floor of the tree house. Whoever threw those water balloons had good aim.

Four Girl Scouts in uniforms popped out from behind the bushes. "This is war, Donald," shouted Susan. "We're coming up to take over the fort. CHARGE!" bellowed Susan as she motioned her Girl Scout troop to follow.

"Oh, no, you're not," yelled Donald. "Quick, Matt, pull up the rope ladder. We can't let those dumb girls come up here."

Matt and Donald grabbed for the rope ladder. But they were too late. Before long, all four Scouts had made their way up the ladder. Donald thought, "Girl Scouts can be very strong because they go on hikes and climb and play lots of sports." Susan was very strong. She almost always beat Donald in arm wrestling. Donald claimed that she cheated by tickling him.

There was lots of pushing and shoving in the tree house.

"Good work, everybody," Susan said quickly. "We did it. I DECLARE THIS TREE HOUSE TO BELONG TO SCOUT TROOP Ninety-nine," she bellowed at the top of her lungs.

In her excitement over this momentous victory, Susan failed to watch her step. She was so excited at her success that she never noticed the fresh banana peel that Donald had thrown aside onto the tree house floor. She slipped and fell sideways over the low rail of the tree house. A lower branch of the large oak broke her fall somewhat but Susan still fell with a terrible thud onto the ground underneath the tree house.

Susan screamed and then began to cry. Donald and Matt and the other Scouts looked over the tree house wall in horror. The accident had occurred so quickly that no one knew exactly what had happened. One Scout began to accuse Matt of pushing Susan. Another one pointed her finger at Donald.

"Stop, stop," said Matt.

The girls were not used to his deaf voice and became suddenly quiet.

Matt began to climb down the rope ladder to Susan, who lay still. Donald quickly followed, with the Scouts coming behind him.

Donald's father had pulled into the driveway. He had heard his daughter scream from the street. Two policemen in a black-and-white car were close behind. They, too, had heard Susan's scream.

"Donald? Susan?" Mr. Dunbar cried out in an anxious tone as he rushed over to the tree.

"My leg! My leg!" wailed Susan. "I can't move it!"

CHAPTER TEN
Pet Wash

It was a pleasant Kentucky afternoon in April. The redbuds up and down the street bloomed with purple flowers.

Susan sat on the front porch with her leg in a cast propped up on a pillow. On her lap sat Merlin, lost in a drowsy sleep. Susan was getting awfully tired of having her leg in a cast. But it had been broken in three places and the doctors told her that she would just have to be patient.

Donald had felt awful about his sister's accident, but even Susan had to admit that it wasn't his fault. It had not been a good idea to try to take his tree house away from him.

Mrs. Dunbar had been very upset: "If you children could learn to get along better, this sort of accident wouldn't happen," she lectured them. "I want you to declare a truce. And I'm serious."

So a truce had been declared, and both children tried a little harder not to lose their tempers. Donald even let Susan be part of the Flying Fingers Club, sometimes.

Right now, Susan watched Donald and Matt, who were on the porch intently writing on some poster board with thick marker pens.

"What are you two up to?" she asked.

"We're getting ready for our pet wash," answered Donald in a tone that tried to be pleasant. But he didn't want Susan messing in. Even with a cast on her leg, and the truce, she was still pretty bossy.

"What in the world is a pet wash?" asked Susan. "I've heard of car washes before but never of pet washes."

Both boys continued to write on the poster board. Donald raised his head, then pushed his glasses back onto his nose and replied, "That's right. It's just like a car wash, but you wash pets, not cars." Donald thought if he just told her she was right she would stop bugging them.

Susan knew she was bothering her brother by his annoyed tone of voice. She remembered her promise about the truce. She tried another approach. "Donald, will you sign my cast? Everyone else has."

"I don't want to," replied Donald, as he continued his printing on the poster board. He pretended he didn't care.

"Please. You're my brother. And Matt can, too," she added.

"Well, okay, if you really want me to," Donald said. He was secretly pleased. He motioned Matt over to Susan's chair. He leaned over and signed his name on the white plaster, printing in large letters.

DONALD

"Hey, nice job," said Susan. "You didn't reverse any letters this time."

Donald had been in Mrs. Brice's learning disabilities class for six months now, receiving tutoring in reading, writing, and spelling. Donald smiled to himself. He knew he had made progress. He could read more easily and write better, too. He had learned lots of interesting stuff from Mrs. Brice. He thought she was the best teacher in the world!

Next Matt signed his name. He drew a heart around it and smiled at Susan. Susan looked at him with surprise.

Donald looked at the heart and glared at Matt. "C'mon, we've got work to do!"

Matt held up the poster for Susan to read.

PET WASH
BIG DOG WASH—25¢
LITTLE DOG WASH—15¢
BLOW DRY —10¢ EXTRA

After setting up their sign in the front yard, the boys filled a big tub with water from the garden hose. Donald went into the house for sponges, towels, his mother's hair dryer, and some soap. He connected the hair dryer to an extension cord. Then the boys sat on the front steps and waited for customers.

One hour went by. Then two. Just when the boys were feeling discouraged, two fire fighters walked by with their Dalmation. "Hey, Jake, look here, a new business in town. Think Spot needs a wash?" said one to the other.

"Sure, why not," said the other man.

Matt ran to the hose to put more water in the tub while Donald emptied in some soap.

They began to lather up the dog and were surprised to see how much he liked the water. The dog wagged his tail as the boys hosed him down.

Jake the fire fighter said, "Spot loves the water. He likes to play in the water when we drain the fire hydrant at the station. I think he's part water rat if you ask me!"

Matt rubbed and rubbed and rubbed. He signed to Donald, "I can't get the spots off. I can't get them off. What do I do?"

The fire fighters stared at the boys using sign language.

Donald explained to Matt, "Those spots are supposed to be there. They don't come off."

When they were through, the men thanked the boys and gave them a dollar bill. "Keep the change, fellas," one fire fighter said to the boys. "And come visit us down at the station. Anytime. And you too, missy, you on the porch, you come with 'em."

By late afternoon the boys were exhausted. They had washed six dogs, some of whom were a struggle. Not all dogs like water, they discovered.

"Look," signed Matt. "Another one."

Sure enough, a woman with a little Scottish terrier was coming toward them. She had lots of hair piled messily on the top of her head, and wore what looked like layers of makeup.

"My, my, what do we have here? A pet wash, how very clever," she said. "How long does this take?" she asked the boys. "I have an appointment at the beauty parlor in forty minutes. Can you fit me in?"

"Oh, we're quick," said Donald.

"Well, the price is right. I think my precious Scottie needs a shampoo. Go ahead if you can be quick about it. Skip the blow dry. It's warm enough for him to dry in the sun. Besides, he has some natural wave. And please be gentle with my precious poopsy-woopsy."

Merlin, who was minding his own business, was chasing flies on the front porch and keeping Susan company. When the terrier saw Merlin, he began to snarl and show his teeth. When Merlin saw the terrier, he suddenly arched his back and began to hiss.

"Oh," said the lady. "You keep cats? I'd never have them in my house in a million years! Scottie has always hated cats, too. We're both allergic to them."

Susan leaned over and gently scooped Merlin into her arms. "Now calm down," she said. Merlin relaxed and curled up into her lap.

The boys lathered the dog, with little cooperation from the terrier.

"Ow," said Donald. "Hey, watch out!" A thin red scratch appeared on Donald's arm where the dog had grazed him with his sharp front teeth.

"Oh, Scottie would *never* bite anyone. Unless, of course, someone bit him first," said the woman as she reapplied her lipstick.

After wrestling with the pooch in the tub of soapy water, Matt took some fresh water from the bucket and rinsed him off. Donald picked up the towel and together the boys gently dried off the terrier, who barked all the while.

Finally, the racket got too much for Merlin. HISS! MEOW! HISS! screeched Merlin as he jumped off Susan's lap and ran toward the boys and Scottie. The dog, sensing the attack, slipped out of the boys' hands and rushed toward the cat. But not until he fell into a mud puddle created by the pet wash activities. Not letting a little mud stop him, the dog rushed Merlin. Growls came from the dog and howls from the cat.

"Oh, my poor little dog. My poor Scottie," the woman wailed.

Fur flew. Legs and tails were tangled into each other. Susan hopped off the porch and down the stairs on one leg and picked up the water hose. She turned on the water and aimed at the two fighting animals. After a few good squirts, the animals had enough. The dog took off down the street with his owner running after, and Merlin skyrocketed up a tree. And it wasn't any tree, but the *tallest* tree in the yard!

"Now what are we going to do?" cried Donald. "That's the tallest tree on the block. We'll never get him down."

Three heads arched toward the sky. Up on the topmost limb sat Merlin, a plump mass of shivering fur.

"C'mon down, Merlin. That awful dog is gone," coaxed Susan.

"How about some cat chow?" promised Donald.

"Merlin, Merlin, come down," signed Matt.

But the black cat wouldn't budge. It wasn't that he didn't want to come down. Sitting on Susan's soft lap was much better than clinging to the rough bark of this stupid tree. But Merlin was scared. Why, he was as high as the birds! He had climbed too far, and now he didn't know how to get back down.

"I've got an idea," said Susan. She hobbled back up the stairs, across the porch, and into the house. She was gone about five minutes while the boys continued to coax Merlin to return to the ground.

Susan returned to the front yard and with confidence she reported, "Problem solved, boys. Leave it to a Girl Scout not to panic and to come through with a solution."

"Susan, what are you talking about?" questioned Donald.

Susan just smiled.

But the boys did not have to wait long for an answer. In just a few minutes, a big red fire engine came down the street.

In lickety-split time the fire fighters erected a ladder that reached to the top of the tree and retrieved the poor, frightened animal.

"What a fat cat," the fire fighter who had earlier given the boys a dollar said as he handed Merlin to Donald. "What are you feeding it, pizza and chocolate cake?"

CHAPTER ELEVEN
The Deal

"Now, what's going on with you guys? You tell us," said Pete, pushing Donald against the wall. Pete and Roger and their friends had surrounded Donald and Matt at school and obviously wanted some information. The boys didn't know what they were talking about. They only knew that the fifth-graders looked mean, and they didn't want to be beaten up.

"Tommy here lives on your street," said Pete, giving Donald a shake. "And he said that there's always a police car parked across the street, and yesterday you had a fire, because he saw the truck, and then he heard a dog fight. . . . And what's all that stuff that you and this guy always do with your fingers? Do you do stuff for the police? We've heard that sometimes the FBI recruits kids to find out about what really goes on in neighborhoods, and like that."

If Donald hadn't been scared, he would have laughed. The reason that there was a police car parked across the street so often was because Sergeant Oliver *lived* across the street. And all the rest was just stuff the guys were making up.

But right now he had to get out of this fix. Why not tell Pete and his friends what they wanted to hear? It would serve them right for being such bullies and always picking on the little kids.

"Well, yes," Donald said slowly. "We are sort of involved with the FBI. But we're sworn to secrecy and can't say anything."

"What do you mean?" snarled Pete. "We're your buddies, right? You can tell us."

"Some terrific friends," Donald thought. Aloud, he said, "Well, Matt here. He's the real FBI agent. All this finger stuff that we're doing. Well . . . it's . . . a . . . secret code." By now Donald was almost whispering.

The other boys were very impressed. "Wow!" said Pete in awe.

"So what are you working on? A drug bust? Or a spy ring? Or *murder*?" asked one boy who watched a lot of TV.

"And do you need any more agents?" asked another boy eagerly.

"I don't know. Let me talk with Matt," replied Donald. "Privately," he added.

Donald motioned Matt to walk with him to the edge of the playground.

"Well," demanded Pete when they returned. "What's up? What did he say?"

Donald paused for a minute. He scratched his head and pushed his glasses up his nose. They had an annoying habit of slipping down. "You have to pass a test," answered Donald in a low voice.

"A test," exclaimed the boys in unison.

"This isn't a school deal, what do you mean by test?" snapped Pete.

"Okay, if you're not interested, then forget it," said Donald as he firmly folded his arms on his chest.

"Who says we're not interested?" said Roger. "It's just that most of us guys don't do too good with the books. We got more important things to think about."

Donald went on. He knew he had the boys hooked. "It's not your ordinary paper and pencil test. This test means you have to do something."

"Like a dare?" asked Roger.

"Kind of like that," replied Donald. "Only a little bit different."

"All right, shrimp," snapped Pete. "Spit it out. We don't have all day," he said impatiently.

"Now watch it, Pete," warned Roger. "These guys work for the FBI. They might have grenades in their backpacks."

"If you all pass the test, well, then we'll write Washington, D.C., to process your papers and send you badges," said Donald.

"Great!" said some of the boys.

But Pete was skeptical. "Show us *his* papers and badge. How do we know you aren't putting us on?" Pete pointed to Matt.

"He has 'em. But they're home," said Donald.

Then Donald explained the test. All had to agree or he and Matt would not go through with it.

That afternoon at recess the boys did not charge to the baseball diamond as they usually did on warm days. Instead, the six fifth-grade boys and Donald and Matt were found under a tree in a grassy corner behind the school. Donald was demonstrating the manual alphabet and Matt was showing the boys a few signs.

"You make *A* like this?" asked Pete.

"What's this sign mean?" demanded Roger.

Suddenly Matt nudged Donald and pointed to the tan backpack on the ground.

"Hey, Pete," said Donald. "Where did you get that backpack?"

"I dunno. I found it lying around somewhere," he answered vaguely.

Then the bell rang to return to school. As Matt and Donald watched the fifth-graders heading for their class, they were as excited as if they really were with the FBI! This was going to work—they'd show those guys.

CHAPTER TWELVE
Day of Silence

"Attention, please. Attention, please." The voice of Mrs. Lake, the principal, came through the loud-speaker. "As we have been planning all month, Mayor Collins will visit our school this afternoon. He will speak on citizenship. All students will assemble in the auditorium at two-fifteen. After the mayor's talk, we will be honored by some selections from our Glee Club. Homeroom teachers please accompany your students. Glee Club members will be excused from class fifteen minutes early to prepare for their performance. Thank you and have a good day."

While the principal made the announcement, Terry interpreted the words for Matt. Donald and the other students sat quietly working on their math.

Mr. Gebhart was at his desk correcting papers. He looked up and said, "Anyone here in Glee Club?"

No one raised a hand.

"Mr. Gebhart," said a boy in the back row, "my brother is in Glee Club, but he's in the fifth grade. I don't think anyone younger than that is in it."

Down the hall in the fifth-grade classroom, the same question was being asked. When the teacher asked who was in Glee Club, up went the hands of Pete, Roger, Tommy, and several other of their friends, as well as a group of girls.

The boys had joined the Glee Club that year not because they loved to sing but so they could get out of an extra music class. They didn't want to have to listen to classical music.

Pete fingerspelled to Roger. Roger fingerspelled back to Pete. Suddenly, all six boys were fingerspelling and signing back and forth to each other. They had been practicing steadily for two weeks with Donald and Matt.

"What is going on?" asked their teacher. "Are you playing some kind of game? I hope you're not cheating on your math assignment!"

Six heads shook no.

When the bell rang, the boys walked into the hallway. They practiced signing and fingerspelling to each other.

At lunchtime, the six boys and Donald and Matt sat together. Signs and fingerspelling flew across the table. No one used his voice. The two weeks of practice had paid off!

Several teachers looked over in disbelief. There were no flying straws, no soggy milk cartons being stepped on and exploded, and no fights over desserts. Were the boys sick? Why, they were even using sign language!

Mr. Primm, the Glee Club director, came running over to the table, out of breath. "Oh, there you are, boys. One fourth of my Glee Club and all sitting together. What luck. Look, fellas, I want you to come a little bit earlier this afternoon before our performance for the mayor. There are a few rough spots in 'Yankee Doodle Dandy' that we need to smooth out. I've already checked with your home-room teacher and she said it was okay."

The boys all nodded in silence at the lunch table. All that could be heard was one boy munching a potato chip.

"Something strange is going on. What's up? Boys, did you hear me?"

Silence. Mr. Primm was surprised that there was no wisecrack from Pete.

"Boys?" he tried again.

Now he was getting angry. "Are you deaf or something?" He then looked at Matt, and, knowing that he was a deaf boy, Mr. Primm retracted his statement.

"Uh . . . I didn't mean that. What I meant, well . . . uh . . . I mean. I MEAN YOU MUST SHOW UP FOR THAT EARLY REHEARSAL," he shouted in an angry and frustrated voice.

Silence at the table.

Mr. Primm ran off with an angry red face. He returned with Mrs. Lake and Terry.

"Now, boys," said Mrs. Lake in a low, firm voice. "What's going on here? Mr. Primm says that you are acting disrespectfully to him. Is this true?"

Still silence.

The principal turned to Terry. "Please ask Matt what's going on," she asked.

Terry and Matt began signing rapidly to each other.

Before the boys knew it, they had been herded into Mrs. Lake's office. She closed the office door and told them all to sit down on the rug because there weren't enough chairs to go around.

"Now, what's going on here? I want to know all about it," Mrs. Lake said sternly.

All the boys started talking at once. "Joke . . . FBI . . . picked on us . . . passing a test . . ." were some of the words that the principal could pick out.

"Hold it, please," said Mrs. Lake. "Donald, I'd like an explanation from you first."

Donald was very aware of the fifth-graders staring at him as he started to talk. "Well," he started slowly. "I guess Matt and I were mad because these guys sometimes picked on us. We thought of a great way to get back at them."

And Donald told the whole story, in detail. About how part of the test was for the boys not to speak at all—just to sign. Singing in the Glee Club would be out of the question, of course. Donald apologized. He hadn't known about the Glee Club performance.

"It seems to me, Donald, that you have concocted a very complicated plot here. I admire your imagination, and I don't doubt for a minute that these fifth-graders were giving you a hard time. But I think we have to consider the school now. We must make a good impression on the mayor. And, boys," she said, looking at the fifth-graders, "Mr. Primm needs you for his program this afternoon, and I expect you to be there on time, and singing."

Everyone filed out, feeling a little silly—Pete and his gang for having been fooled; Donald for having caused so much trouble. Mrs. Lake had been very nice about it, but Donald and Matt hoped that the fifth-graders would be as forgiving.

CHAPTER THIRTEEN

Where the Chili Sauce Clue Led

Bees buzzed around the tulips and daffodils flowering on the side of the playground. Donald and Matt, in T-shirts and shorts sat against a tree trunk during recess discussing the coming end of the school year.

"So, what are you going to do this summer?" signed Donald to Matt.

"We're going to the beach. I can't wait to body surf the waves at the ocean. I just love it! What about you?"

"Mom wants to go study soils in the Southwest, so she's dragging us across the country, the whole family. I'd really prefer to stay here and play baseball."

"But going on a trip across the country sounds fun," signed Matt back to Donald.

"Well, maybe," signed Donald. "Look who's coming over here!"

Pete and Roger were walking toward the boys.

"Hey, you guys, what's up?" said Pete in a

friendly tone. Ever since the showdown in the principal's office, Pete had been oddly friendly to Donald and Matt. The principal had issued an ultimatum that the boys would be civil to each other on school property. Or else.

"Oh, nothing much," said Donald warily. He didn't feel comfortable with Pete.

"Look what I have here," Pete said as he pulled off his tan backpack. "It's the school newspaper, and look whose story is on the back page."

"Why, it's mine!" Donald beamed with pride. "It's a story I did on the computer. I didn't know that Mrs. Brice was going to send it in!" he said and jumped up and down. He showed the paper to Matt.

Matt looked at the paper, then looked at Pete's backpack. "Chili sauce!" he signed to Donald.

"What? What did you say? Matt, look at my story!" signed Donald with impatience.

Pete had become a little uneasy. "You can keep it. I gotta go now," he said. He picked up his backpack and walked away.

"Matt, don't you even care about my story?" said Donald.

"It's not that, but the chili sauce all down the side of the bag, doesn't that mean anything to you?" signed Matt with disgust. "Think of the Bluegrass Diner. There are bowls of it all over the place. It's their specialty. They make their own!"

That afternoon, Matt, Donald, and Susan met in the tree house. "So what's the emergency meeting all about?" asked Susan.

"Matt here thinks that Pete is the newspaper thief," said Donald. "On account of the chili sauce on the tan backpack."

"But we have no real proof. We're still missing parts of this puzzle," said Susan thoughtfully. We need the red ski cap and we need . . . a confession from the crook. If we accuse him outright, he could deny it. After all, the chili sauce may not have come from the Bluegrass Diner. And lots of people own tan backpacks. Hmm . . . how could we find out if he owns a red ski cap?" asked Susan.

"We could call and ask his mother." said Donald.

"No," signed Matt. "That would warn him. He could destroy the evidence."

"How about getting him to go with us to the Bluegrass and see if anyone there recognizes him?" added Donald.

"No," said Susan. "He'd know something was up and refuse to come."

The kids thought for a while.

"I know," exclaimed Susan. "Let's have an end-of-the-school-year party at our house and we'll have a scavenger hunt. And one of the items people have to get will be a red ski cap. Then when Pete shows up with the red cap, we'll nail him!"

So the three detectives of the Flying Fingers Club planned a party with a scavenger hunt. They would each invite several friends, including Susan's Girl Scout buddies, much to Matt and Donald's chagrin. The fact that these girls had stormed the tree house was not easily forgotten.

Two Saturdays later, on the day of the party, Susan, Donald, and Matt were busy setting up the refreshments in the Dunbars' backyard.

"Put that pitcher of lemonade over on the picnic table, Donald, and be sure to put a cover on it, so no bugs will drop in," ordered Susan. "And don't open the potato chips just yet. Wait until we are ready to eat or they'll get stale," she continued.

Donald clenched his teeth. No matter how well he and Susan got along these days, she was still going to order him around. He had the feeling it would last until she went away to college!

"Let's see," went on Susan in her bossy way. "Here's the list. Tell me what you think of it. The kids must find: one, the inside of a golf ball; two, a happy meal box from McDonald's; three, one *Star Trek* comic book and it can't be new!; four, one pine cone; five, one ski cap, preferably red; six, one bottle top from a Coke; seven, one seashell; and eight, one corn cob pipe. We'll give the kids thirty minutes to find these things in the neighborhood, then we'll all meet back here and whoever gets the most in the time permitted will win the prize."

"What's the prize?" asked Donald.

"Two tickets to the movies," replied Susan. "Matt's parents donated them because Mom and Dad provided the refreshments for the party."

When the kids arrived, they sat around the picnic table and chattered about their plans for summer vacation. Some were going to camp and others were staying in town or visiting relatives. After they had stuffed themselves with chips, cookies, and candy, and washed it down with lemonade, Susan organized the scavenger hunt.

"And, finally," said Susan as she finished giving the instructions, "meet back here in exactly thirty minutes with your items. I will be here to record who comes in first, second, third, and so forth." Susan gave everyone a list of items.

The half hour passed quickly. Pete was the first one to return. He had all the items. "Wonderful!" thought Susan excitedly to herself. "He has the red ski cap. We've got him!" But when the others came back, she found that three other kids had red ski caps, too! It seemed that red ski caps had been the fashion that winter.

"What are we going to do?" said Susan to Donald and Matt in a dejected manner. There was nothing *to* do but award Pete the prize. No one else had found every item.

"Well, thanks for the prize, guys," said Pete a little later as he got ready to leave.

"Pete, we want to ask you something," announced Donald. He couldn't stand it anymore. He had decided to confront Pete. "We think that from time to time you stole Susan's papers on Sunday mornings and then sold them to the Bluegrass Diner!" he blurted out.

"Hey, you kids are jerks after all. You can't prove anything."

"Look, last winter we saw the thief leave on a bike with a red ski cap and holding a tan backpack. And the chili sauce on your backpack . . . I bet it comes right from the diner. There are always bowls of it around. We think it's you!" said Donald confidently.

"You have no proof. Lots of kids have red caps. And lots of kids have tan backpacks. As for the chili sauce, well, any turkey knows that you can get chili sauce at any restaurant. So there," he continued angrily.

"Well, we tried to get the people at the diner to identify you, but—"went on Susan.

"Ah, ha, so there," taunted Pete. "I'm splitting."

Donald nudged Matt, who reached into his pocket and pulled out something. "Well, what about this?" said Donald in an accusatory tone.

Matt help up a gold key chain with some initials on it.

"So, what does that mean?" asked Pete in a weak voice.

Susan didn't know what they were talking about. She was stunned.

"Does it belong to you?" asked Donald.

"No," said Pete in a still weaker voice.

Donald reached over to Matt and turned the key chain over. "Well, I see the initials R. P. Q., Jr. Who could that be?" he said.

"Could be anybody," Pete mumbled.

"Matt and I found this key chain outside the condo complex. Matt had seen it fall out of your pocket last winter, but it had become lost in the snow. We found it today after digging around in the mud. We also checked on all the R. P. Q.'s who live in our town in the phone book." Donald pulled a yellow paper from his pocket. "Let me see. I have here a Richard Philip Quade, who lives in a rest home so he couldn't be the one, and a Ron P. Quarrles. He has no children. The only other R. P. Q. in the phone book is a Robert Peter Quinn, Sr. Do you know who he is?" asked Donald.

"Yeah," mumbled Pete. "It's my father."

"So the key chain does belong to you!" exclaimed Susan.

"Okay, okay, I did it. I needed the money. I wanted to get a new Walkman," he said.

"Well, you owe our parents about ninety dollars for all the newspapers they had to buy," said Donald. "And if you don't pay up, we're going to call the cops," he continued.

"Look, I'll pay. I'll pay. I'll come over this weekend and give your folks the dough," said Pete.

"When we get our money, then we'll give you back your key chain," said Donald as he folded his arms across his chest.

"Do you want the movie tickets back?" Pete asked.

"No, you won those," said Susan. "But we want the money for the newspapers!"

Pete looked down at his feet and turned away and left.

"The jerk didn't even say he was sorry," said Donald.

"He's probably wondering where he's going to get all that money," signed Matt.

"Hey, Don?" said Susan.

"Yeah, Sue?" replied Donald.

"Thanks," she said.

"What about me?" asked Matt, smiling.

"Thanks to you, too," she said.

That night, at dinner, Donald and Susan described their adventures.

"Sherlock Holmes would be proud!" their mother said. "And so am I."

CHAPTER
FOURTEEN
The
Spelling
Bee

The school year was just about over. Even the pink blossoms on the dogwood trees had turned to green leaves, signaling the end of springtime and the coming of summer. As Donald and Matt had requested, a sign club was initiated at Lincoln with Terry agreeing to help teach signs and finger-spelling to the other children at the school. Not surprisingly, Pete and Roger left them strictly alone, especially after Pete had repaid the debt to Mr. and Mrs. Dunbar. Susan's paper route con-tinued uninterrupted and was doing so well that she was thinking of expanding it.

"Don't forget about the family's summer plans," her mother warned. "Remember, we are all going to the Southwest on a soil-digging expedition. Your route will have to wait until fall."

Despite the impending separation that the summer would inevitably bring, Donald felt very close to Matt. There were many private jokes that they had shared over the school year. They had had good times together.

But, still, life was not easy for Matt at Lincoln Elementary.

"Matt, come sit at our table," said two girls one day in the cafeteria. "Matt, Matt," they repeated.

But Matt did not hear the girls. He was facing them but not looking at them, so he walked on by.

"Oh, he's so stuck up," said one of the girls.

"He is not," defended Donald, who was standing near and overheard the conversation.

"Forget it," said the girls, and went back to their sandwiches.

"People are always forgetting that you can't hear," said Donald to Matt. "They want to learn a few signs but seem to lose interest when they have to use it with you. Who cares about them! I just love sign language and using my hands to talk."

Donald was getting better and better at signing. He wished his other schoolwork would go as well. Still, he was improving, and one day he surprised everyone, including himself.

During the last week of the school year, Mr. Gebhart invited some boys and girls from other classrooms to participate in the class annual end-of-the-year spelling bee.

While Team A and Team B assembled in front of the classroom, getting ready for the event, other children from the lower grades came to watch. Terry was standing in the back of the room with Matt.

Mr. Gebhart started the spelling match. "All right, boys and girls, you'll be given only fifteen seconds to spell each word. Now, Donald, you'll be first."

A girl on Donald's team leaned over to another girl nearby. "Well, we can forget about this point. Donald's in Mrs. Brice's dumbbell class. He can't spell worth beans!"

"Okay, Donald, spell the word 'exercise,'" said Mr. Gebhart.

All eyes were fixed on Donald. Some of the kids on the other team smiled at each other.

Donald looked at his friend Matt at the back of the room. Donald shut his eyes. In his mind, he pictured lots of letters. But the letters were all in a jumble! How should he order them? Donald felt panic-stricken.

"Five seconds," said Mr. Gebhart while looking at his stopwatch.

Donald's fingers uncurled from a tight fist at his side. His relaxed fingers seemed to move by themselves, forming the letter handshape "e," followed by the other handshapes "x-e-r-c-i-s-e." He blurted out loud these letters in order, using his fingers as a guide.

"Correct," said Mr. Gebhart in a surprised voice.

Donald's team let out a whoop. Donald looked at his friend Matt and smiled. Matt gave Donald the thumbs-up sign.

Even though Donald's team did not win the spelling bee that day, they came awfully close to the other team.

"Hey, Donald," said Mr. Gebhart after the

spelling bee. "You did all right for yourself. You ought to keep up with that fingerspelling. It seems to help you sometimes."

"Yeah," replied Donald, with pleasure. "Matt has helped me out a lot, you know. I've learned a lot of stuff."

"Well, keep up the good work, Donald," said Mr. Gebhart.

CHAPTER FIFTEEN
A Talk About Friendship

"What do you mean, you aren't coming back to Lincoln!" Donald shouted and signed to Matt in anger.

"My parents said that I could go back to the deaf school next year if I wanted and that's what I want to do," replied Matt calmly.

"But you have it good around here! Many of the boys and girls know signs, Terry is always around, the teachers like you. You can even spell better than me. I know you just hate us, that's what's wrong!" Donald was holding back the tears.

"That's not it and you know it, Donald," explained Matt. "It's just that I'm tired of being different. I want to be with kids more like me, that's all! And I'm tired of always getting stuck."

"What do you mean, stuck?" asked Donald.

"Remember when I was left behind during the fire drill last week? I was in the restroom washing my hands after art class and when I returned, the classroom was empty because everyone had gone outside for the fire drill. Then when I walked outside, everybody laughed at me. Has that ever happened to you, Donald, where a whole school laughed at you?" he asked.

Matt's signing was so strong that it made Donald uncomfortable just watching it.

"I miss my teachers at the deaf school, too," added Matt.

"But the deaf school is so far away!" said Donald.

"It's only a two-hour drive. And I'll come home on weekends. That way I can go out for sports and join the drama club," he signed.

"I know, you told me that before," Donald said sadly.

"Deaf school is better. . . ." Matt began his tirade again about how much he preferred the deaf school.

"OH SHUT UP! JUST SHUT UP," yelled Donald. "I'm tired of you always saying, 'Deaf is better,' 'Deaf is better,' 'Deaf is better.' You make me want to throw up. I never want to see you again. You're not my friend anymore. Go find some other deaf friends if you think they are so great. I hate you! I hate you! I hate you!"

By now, Donald was crying out loud. Matt walked away to another part of the playground.

"Is anything wrong?" said Mrs. Brice as she ran over to Donald. She had recess duty and was observing the boys' quarrel from across the playground.

"I want to go home. I feel sick," cried Donald.

Mrs. Brice could not stop Donald's tears. She tried to comfort him. "Donald, let's go in so you can lie down a bit." She led the unhappy boy into the school building. "Do you want to talk about what happened?" she asked.

"No, I can't!" Donald wailed. Mrs. Brice had the good sense not to press the issue. So he lay on the couch in the teachers' room until the end of the school day. When he got on the bus to go home, he sat in the back, making sure Matt was not near.

When Donald got home, he went straight to his bedroom and went to sleep. His parents and Susan did not wake him up for dinner. They had received a phone call from Mrs. Brice telling them that Donald was not feeling too well.

Donald's mother noticed something was still wrong with her son the next morning.

"Donald, what are you doing with that large bag of candy?" she said as she saw her son standing on a stool reaching into the kitchen cabinet.

Donald had a jumbo bag of candy bars and was stuffing it into his backpack. "I'm taking this candy to school."

"Sweetie, you can't eat all that candy for lunch, you'll make yourself sick," said his mother in a concerned voice.

"It's not for me," Donald said. "I'm gonna give it to Matt so he'll want to stay at Lincoln next year."

"Donald, are you trying to bribe him?" she asked.

Angry tears rolled down Donald's face.

His mother put down her purse and schoolbooks. "Donald, why don't we go for a little walk."

Then, between the tears and heaves and heaves and more tears, Donald explained to his mother

Matt's plans to return to the state school for the deaf. He told her how hard it was for him to make friends, especially after the family had moved from Illinois and he had to say good-bye to Jackie. Now he'd finally found a good friend in Matt, but Matt was leaving him.

"Yes, I sympathize with you," said his mother softly. "I know it must have been hard on both you and Susan to move and have to start all over."

Donald sniffed some more.

"Really, son," said his mother. "Giving people *things* like candy is not a way to keep friends. Gifts are for celebrating friendships. Besides, just because Matt leaves Lincoln doesn't mean he'll stop being your friend."

"But I want a close friend that I get to see every-day," complained Donald. "And that's what Matt has been all this school year!"

"Yes, I do understand," she said. "But you'll see Matt," continued his mother as they walked around the corner. "He only lives a few blocks away. You'll see him on weekends. It's not as if he's moving to another state. Why don't we throw him a party? A good-bye-but-not-really-good-bye party?"

"No, I don't want to have a party," said Donald as another big tear rolled down his cheek. "The party will only remind me of losing him and it will make me feel even more sad."

On the morning of the last day of school, Donald saw Matt at the drinking fountain. He walked over to him.

"Donald," signed Matt as he wiped his dripping

mouth with the back of his hand. "I've been looking all over for you."

"I've been looking for you, too," signed Donald slowly. "Look, I'm sorry . . . about . . ."

Matt interrupted and began to sign excitedly. "Why don't you come visit me at the state school for the deaf for a week next school year?"

"How could I do that? I'd have school here at Lincoln. I just couldn't play hooky for a whole week! My parents would never let me!" he replied.

"You don't have to," began Matt. "I've already checked it out with my mother. You see, my school starts two weeks earlier than Lincoln. We start on August seventeenth and Lincoln doesn't start until September first."

"Lucky us," signed Donald.

"Yeah," replied Matt. "But what I was saying was you can come stay with me during the last week of August, from the twenty-first to the thirtieth. That'll give you two weekends at the school. You can come to class with me, then we're going on a camping trip on the weekend of the twenty-eighth. It's going to be two nights out at Cumberland Falls with a white-water raft trip and everything!"

"Cumberland Falls! Cumberland Falls! I've never been there," said Donald, bouncing on his toes. "Are you sure I could come?"

"Yes. Dad asked about it when he reenrolled me. The dorm counselor at my dorm just happens to be his former roommate from college. He's going to work on all the arrangements." Matt clapped his hands and punched Donald on the arm in an affectionate way.

"Whoopee!" shouted Donald.

"And, Donald," added Matt. "I was saving the best part until last."

"What's that?" asked Donald.

"It's about my old dormitory, where I'm living next year," answered Matt.

"Well, what about it?" asked Donald, getting more curious by the moment.

Matt put his arm around Donald and turned him to the wall. Then he bent his head and signed low near Donald's chest so no one could see what he wanted to communicate. "There is a secret trapdoor in the attic of the boy's dormitory that we just *have* to explore."

Donald could hardly wait.